I0589672

ISBN: 978-1087-9100-5

Dedicated to great Asian people everywhere.

# Table of Contents

# THE KONG FLUE CHRONICLES

## 'Ezra's Dark Sunny Side'

Ezra was engaged in an infernal battle of wits-all her own. Trouble was afoot, that much was certain, as certain as the hissing racket of her steaming teapot, which she ignored. Perched on a small table next to the stovetop was her cat, 'Vigilance', fixated on the diminutive, elderly lady figure, perched, herself, on her usual non-descript kitchen chair by the 2nd floor tenement window, peering through her drawn blinds-sneaking a peek-at the bright, sunny day outside. Inside the sparse apartment, it may have been dusk, gray and dismal.

"Hello. I'd like to report suspicious activity," Ezra lamented, over the phone.

"And what *activity* would that be?" the uniformed precinct desk cop asked her. He nudged his sergeant, sitting astride, nodded, and they both broke out in wide grins. Ezra was a *regular.*

"There is a man walking a dog under my window," Ezra declared.

Officer Littsom nearly lost his coffee.

"And is the dog presently on a leash, I presume, ma'am?" he asked politely.

"Well...yes, it is on a leash," she continued, "but, I'm not familiar with these two...and the man looks like a foreigner to me," Ezra insisted.

The officer's chuckled under their breath.

"Why aren't they under quarantine, and why must they be HERE, in the first place?" Ezra flicked the blind upward, deftly, with her index finger to offer a better view below, yet, not so high as to arouse suspicion. The man looked up, anyway, so Ezra, reflexively, withdrew her finger quickly, snapping the blind shut. Vigilance bared her fangs, soundlessly, from her own perch, offering a desultory twitch of the tail.

"I think he just SAW me!" Ezra decried. "What are you going to DO about it?"

About WHAT?" Officer Littsom asked.

Little Ezra stomped her foot and the cat jumped. The teapot rattled on, the city crawled at a snail's pace, and the neighborhood lady kept careful watch on the slightest of movement threatening to derail her senses, entirely.  **THE END**

## 'BEDLAM IN BENSONHURST'

"I'm SICK of this f'ing CRAP!" Gloria shouted, cracking the louvered kitchen slats, like a Vesuvius *Laura Petrie*, gone apoplectic. The men all turned their heads, at once, staring dumbly at the pretty face that glared back.

"Why don't you all go back to your OWN wives, and leave me the heck alone, just for...one...stinking...day!"

Diminutive Gloria was, to put it mildly, livid, as well as being the proverbial sight to behold. Her ample cleavage heaved from a revealing halter, and her signature retro *beehive* bobbed like Carmen Miranda's fruit basket dancing atop her head. The look never changed much, tortuously appealing to the slobs that gathered nightly, at George's place, to play poker. Impassioned anger only enhanced her glow, certainly.

"Now...hon'. Is that anyway to treat my friends?" her husband insisted. He gently kicked a drained can, positioned on the floor for effect, but it clipped the waste basket rim, and fell harmlessly to the floor.

"AWwwwww", his buddies groaned.

An impressive pyramid stack of empties-*Tower of Babel*-awaited, however, propped center-stage on the card table. The men bumped fists to make it dance, a bit, giggling like the "children" they were.

Gloria carefully removed the tray of chicken wings from her oven rack, gave the greasy mess a perfunctory blow-as if to cool a steaming bowl of oatmeal-nudged the swinging half-door open with a deft hip bump and yammered demonstrably toward the men.

"WE ARE IN LOCKDOWN...HERE ARE YOUR CHICKEN WINGS!!!"

They flew off in all directions, grease splattering the walls. A few of George's wolfish pals snatched the magnificent morsels off the floor, hungrily.

"Five second rule in effect!" they clamored.

George's windmill wind-up thrilled the gang, now. He apishly mimed mustachio *Shaw*, pitcher of yore, wheeling a dripping cold one, drawn from the Styrofoam picnic chest parked on the shag rug-all eyes riveted toward the *Tower*. As Gloria glared, hands on hips, with her bewitching *Persian Lilly's*, George stood unwaveringly, for dramatic effect, resolutely undeterred, so to speak, to the delight of the gang, holding their collective breaths, in suspended animation.

The *Tower* was laid waste then with a flourish...with all the delicacy of milk bottles strewn on a midway, by some Norman brute wielding a medieval flail, in Essex.

The men yelped and were promptly given the heave-ho, sheepishly exiting the front door past Gloria, one-by-one, in customary fashion. They loved their feisty Italian hostess...and she, strangely enough, loved them back, despite it all.  **THE END**

### 'Marcus Rules the Day'

Jet fighters scrambled off the deck of the mighty carrier, as puffs of smoke could be seen far out in the distance, over a shimmering sea of blue. Colonel Marcus adjusted his own snappy helmet, his hands pressed against each side, in preparation for another impressive lift-off. As was usually the case, he imagined himself a gridiron hero, in this transitory moment...THE pivotal figure entering THE game at just the right time-adoring hometown crowd roaring their approval (in reality, the closest the *real* Marcus got to a football field was the time his geeky science pals nearly blew one up, playing with pyrotechnics), as he thrust his helmet on in an, decidedly, truculent manner, triumphant in due course, in due time.

The crowd chanted Marcus! Marcus! He wouldn't disappoint. He would weave and spin and dodge and vault over disjointed defenders, hapless to stem the tide of ultimate victory, and be hoisted on shoulders to the wild screams of bouncy, pom-pom waving cheerleaders (in actuality, he had never dated a girl!)…and he would, suddenly, feel free…

…free as a bird…free as a dolphin breaking stride in a speedboat's wake…

…reveling in that ecstasy of pure, unimpeded motion …of unbridled emotion…goal line approaching fast…then stretching further…Marcus *flying* to the goal line, finally, the game clearly won, NOW!…foregone conclusion, as it were.

The Colonel's *harrier jet* rose distinctively off deck, a singular uplifting sensation, in every regard. He experienced, then, a surge of adrenalin, strapped securely in his cockpit…a feeling of levitation…and then the sudden, inexplicably terrifying drop…and one moment before it………..

"Marcus…MARCUS! WAKE-UP!"

His arms were crossed and he shook in his sleep, violently, like Houdini in a straight-jacket, unable to reach his eject button…then opened his eyes. His doting mother's face was inches away from

9

his own. Dorothy was bent over and dressed to the far side of sixty, in shabby nightgown and a head full of curlers. She was still shaking his bony shoulders, purposefully, appearing shockingly aghast.

"You're dreaming, Marcus-it's time to get up!"

He closed his eye's snap shut, and rolled over with a grunt.

"You're, probably, dreaming of hula girls, dancing on a Waikiki beach," she teased, exuding a matronly giggle. Marcus farted. "Well, you don't have to be CRASS!" Dorothy chuckled.

"Leave me alone, Ma," he replied, sinking deeper into the soft mattress.

"French toast and maple syrup...and fresh squeezed OJ!" Dorothy coaxed, lovingly, in her sweetest morning sing-song voice.

Marcus rolled back over and lunged for his cigarette pack. The pack stood at attention, upright, like an obedient pet, next to a darkened alarm clock that hadn't worked in months.

"Today is going to be the BIG DAY", his mother squealed. "I can feel it!"

He could hear the flip flop of her worn slippers fading as she made her way down the scuffed wooden staircase. Marcus shouted through the wall of his *banner* room, relic of a bygone era-his childhood-that maintained a firm grasp, so to speak, even at forty. He shivered in a room not the least chilly, shaking his skinny legs, convulsively, into furry pajama bottoms, patterned with athletic balls.

"Have you forgotten, Ma... you know...the FLU!" He stood like a tall sentry at the top of the stairs, now.

"Shu-flu-ta-DOO!" Dorothy replied. "Not the FLU, Marcus...it's a VIRUS!"

"Ok, Ma...whatever you say, but, it's still the flu...and I'm not leaving the house."

11

He smiled as an aromatic wave struck, mid-stride, as he went loping across the nondescript living room.

Marcus would spend the day...another day, along a string of weeks...no, months, in similar fashion, locked inside his basement *command post,* furiously working his *mouse.* Breakfast was a mere formality, the computer his life. His screen name became 'Vortex'. He rarely bathed, much to his mother's consternation, but, rather, remained steadfastly ensconced in his cyber dungeon, smoking incessantly, texting madly with his fellow sleuths. The pandemic became grist for the conspiracy mill...lots of *false flag* horseshit going on...Bio-weaponry unleashed...massive transfers of wealth, all befitting the 1%...the phony global shutdown.

"Í worry about your *porn,* Marcus!" Dorothy yelled, from the top of the cellar stairs, sounding like Edith Bunker.

"The world's coming to an end, Ma!" Marcus bellowed back, from his *inner-sanctum*, the basement *bowels.* He chuckled then, before diving into a giant bag of chips and slugging some syrupy soda.

"You've got to watch your health, Marcus!"

"Got a handle on it, Ma!"

If only the masses knew, the lanky man-child surmised. He pounded the desktop, and his keyboard jumped. An incoming text alert chimed. This was the element of sheer nothingness, all in all…his life, basically…and Marcus knew it. **THE END**

### 'PREACHER JONES'

*"Out of the crooked timber of humanity, no straight thing was ever made."*

-Immanuel Kant

"We are held NOT by the norms of conformity, nor crumble in the face of adversity-of perverse society-pouring forth iniquity to drown in sorrow and depraved indifference, or, become ensnared by infernal trappings that lay us low, like cattle led to slaughter, squeezing each and every ounce of God-given purity, until, INDEED, our very entrails spill out on the floor. We will not be deterred, nor acquiesce and enjoin to the failings of modern man...nor, wilt like hydrangea for lack of drink...DRINK people the spring of LIFE...drink not the poison that befalls weak men, that saps the spirit, leaving humankind parched and dry as bleached bones in a desert. Only the Holy Spirit can guide us-indeed, a leavening of bread, as

Covenant, is revealed-a healing spirit so divine as to...not...be... *quarantined*!"

The statuesque Preacher Jones thrust his arms skyward, pumping clenched fists, as the posture perfect organist pounded her furious keys.

"Open up the gates, the people want to come in!" he thundered.

Congregants, young and old, strong and frail, stood in rapt observance, arms raised and waving like gentle wheat in the breeze, adherent to a calling, heads bowed in eternal reverence, and humility, and gratitude and solemnity.

"Bow NOT to the *State* authority, friends!" he warned, as the loyal parishioners nodded in the affirmative. They just as quickly began shaking their heads sideways, in unison, as he railed, "They tell us to STAY HOME! Don't go to church! You'll get sick and spread it around. Was Jesus turned away when he was off doing the healings, giving sight to the blind, I ask? Did someone tell HIM to stay home and watch a game show?" The flock gaggled like geese at that one.

Preacher Jone's formidable hands grasped the lectern, and he began to shake, convulsively, it seemed, shake like a majestic mountain quaking in its boots. Sweat poured forth his prominent brow, not in beads, or rivulets, but, as a cascading river tumbling over rock.

"I, hereby, declare our flock exempt from all whims and fancies of man...if not their *Law* altogether...not to be confused by mere obfuscation of their decrees and detriments, the deadening morass, as you will, but, singularly, to RAISE the Spirit of the living and dead, and REJOICE about it...Hallelujah!

Strains of 'Rock of Ages' poured forth, now, as if on cue.

*'Foul, I to the fountain fly...wash me Savior, or I die.'*

"Friends, be cleansed in the light of God, our Father…go forth in the brightness of day, not drawn like moths to the flame of darkness. Repent and be SAVED, children! Amen."

As the large congregation filed out of the gleaming white church, the moment they hit the steps, they were greeted with angry stares from the sidewalk, catcalls even. Enraged citizen's, arms crossed, lashed out with serpent's tongue, so to speak, in the scorching Florida sun.

"You're going to make us sick!" was the message.

The local sheriff stepped forward and slapped the cuffs.

"We warned you, Reverend."

Preacher Jones stood tall, nevertheless, immoveable in his faith. The virus continued to spread throughout the land, unabated and unchecked. There was no cure at hand, no vaccine. People were told to stay at home, and most complied. Dark times, indeed, for the unwashed multitudes...no cause for alarm bells for others, however, seeking to be healed by an, altogether, *Higher Authority*...drawn to that brilliant ray of light streaking forth through ominous clouds of fearful hysteria, in the worshipper's minds and hearts.

*'As for the one who is weak in faith, welcome him, but not to quarrel over opinions'-Romans 14:1*

*'This is my commandment, that you love one another as I have loved you'*

*John 15:12*

## 'FROM SAG HARBOR, WITH LOVE'

Genevieve and Miguel are the nicest couple you could ever meet. They are middle-aged wage earners with *Green Cards*, from Honduras, have five pleasantly cheerful children, and are both recently laid-off. Jumping on the unemployment gravy train, they find, is tougher to navigate than an isolated gazelle outmaneuvering a pack of hungry cheetahs.

Genevieve surveyed the produce section, as a hedge pruner might view his broader landscape, distinctly, with a clarity of vision, one of halcyon days spent laboring amidst pastoral splendor, of luxuriant fields of plenty. The *greens* accepted the timed spray, a vine tomato rolled the deck on to the floor, and plump pineapple shades kept company with a platoon of fuzzy coconuts...but, her mind drifted back to the meat section. Making the supermarket rounds, she had passed it by, surely to return.

This couple was in a fix, one they weren't at all prepared for (keeping in mind, they were a migrant family that had endured terrific hardship and arduous journey, along the way), as the reeling nation, as a whole, had taken pause-no, slammed the brakes on! The pandemic WAS the deer in the headlights, staring straight ahead.

She was a hard-working chambermaid at a stylishly vintage B & B, on Long Island, quaintly called the 'The Coquettish Conch', cleaning sheets and scrubbing toilets and polishing table tops. He was a landscape *architect.* The "lockdown" had cost them their jobs, for the time being, as late-winter rolled into early spring. School was finished for the foreseeable future, as well.

Their children ranged, in age, from six to fifteen (Genevieve, endearingly, referred to them as her "five little backpacks marching off to class") were, now, stuck at home. Genevieve loved having them there, to watch over and nurture and smother with hugs and kisses. She, assiduously, honed their *English* skills, and relished her newfound role as *homeschool* teacher around the dining room table. Her approach to discipline was to limit gadgetry, of the digital kind. Nothing was more ruinous, in the mom's mind, than the latest video games, and tablets, and cell phones. They spoiled kids, she thought, and were highly addictive. Besides, she couldn't afford all that stuff, anyway. Her children, at least, wouldn't become little, demanding, mechanized robots.

Mild-mannered, doting dad Miguel was equal to the task, at hand, although the rambunctious little one, Tiera, took terrible delight in driving her daddy completely off his *rocker,* at times. Her game of *hide and seek* never stopped. It's all the little six-year old wanted to do all day-between lessons, of course. Keeping the little *charges* in line, scrambling about hither and thither, was a decidedly tricky task, at times, for sure, but, the happy couple managed, somehow, even in these worrisome days of uncertainty and unknowns.

The Mejia's were a cheerful, outgoing family, who loved the idyllic village of Sag Harbor, and the community loved them back, with equal measure. Summer was full of sun-splashed days at the sandy beach-a coastal plain it is-and sprawling picnics spent under their favorite Scarlet Oak tree in the town square, where the kids clamored about the mighty trunk and swung like wild monkeys on gnarly low-hanging branch, watching zippy bluebirds and swallows flit about over their heads...little creatures hopping and darting about, as if in a colorful, motion-filled dreamscape.

Genevieve's mind was a flutter, now, at the market. As this infernal *lockdown,* fragged on, mercilessly, for weeks and, now, MONTHS...things were getting tight. Their savings (if you could call it that), amounted to nil. Nothing was affordable...that juicy rack of ribs she spotted earlier, however, weighed heavily on the mom's mind. It sat there on the upper shelf, surrounded by an assembly of other meaty assortments...that one <u>THERE</u> had her name on it!

She relished these moments, reflectively, just then. Her brain raced too fast, she had to take pause and...just be grateful. Grateful to have a brief respite from the little *charges,* to be alone with her hubby on a relaxing shopping trip. Grateful for her co-worker best friend, and next door neighbor, Delilah, who she took turns with, on occasion, swapping out her kids, for their own.

Miguel raised a hefty cantaloupe, caressingly, off the shelf-twinkle in his eye-giving his wife a playful, mischievous grin.

"I'll be RIGHT BACK!" Genevieve yelped.

She tore down the aisle, sturdy, short maidenly legs churning like pistons past the bottled juices and nuts, whipped the corner-nearly run down by a motorized pallet cart-scampered stealthily beyond other meaningless aisles and stopped dead in her tracks. Like the rug was swept under her feet and she had done a backflip...like she had immersed herself in a sparkling cool pond, only to find her head stuck in a blasted sand pit...gob smacked and gutted. Genevieve gasped. The meat section was empty!

Nothing there...and to make matters worse, she watched helplessly as the *last man standing*-her *muskellunge-sized rib rack* was being tossed, haphazard-like atop a heaping mass mess of a cart...chock full of other meats! Five blasted carts in all!

Her immediate object of scorn and derision stood there with his toned back turned, adjusting the hefty package, precision-like, now, so as not to topple over the side to the floor. She recognized the designer-clad *Hedge Fund* type, from her long days spent slaving over rich folk; thirty-something and insufferably rude, sporting penny loafers and no socks. Alongside his perky blonde girlfriend (texting frantically, of course) appeared a half-dozen foot soldiers, of the yachting kind; his crew, no doubt, dressed uniformly in blue monogrammed anchor muscle shirts, and white slacks.

Genevieve strode defiantly toward him, tapping him on the shoulder rat-a-tat-tat, with the urgency of a distressed Morse code operator. He offered the slightest, nonchalant turn of the head.

"Excuse me, Mister," she said, pointing to his cart, "but, that's my rack of ribs."

He half-turned, as his *Jo Jo-skirted cosmetic job* continued tapping her phone, oblivious of Genevieve.

"Well, obviously, no, it's not," he replied smugly. I think you...should...just...move...on." The yachtsman averted her eyes, altogether. "Let's go," he snapped to his crew, leaving the poor woman standing alone, broken-hearted.

It was to be a last big meal she and Miguel could swing for a while, under the circumstances. Genevieve was at a loss what to do. What would she tell her husband? How could it be possible her *timing* had been so terribly wrong?

The pair exited the store glumly, silent as stones.

What they didn't realize, however...what they were soon to find out, one scratch-off away...was that *Lady Luck,* in her most exasperated of moments, had gazed into the face of her one and only $2 dollar bill-as they parted ways-and Thomas Jefferson had smiled back (he had a particular fondness for maids, after all!).

Genevieve had won the big prize!  **THE END**

*It was as if*...the world had lost its collective mind, in 2020...except for China, of course.

*It was as if*...the virus, perhaps, was an ever-mutating, form of Bio-weaponry unleashed (whether intentional, or, otherwise), which would, ultimately, crash the US economy...and China knew it, beforehand.

*It was as if*...Chinese scientists were kicked out of the National Microbiology Lab, in Winnipeg, Canada, in July 2019, with ties to the Wuhan Institute of Virology, after "a shipment of exceptionally virulent viruses" (see: *'Coronavirus Outbreak a Result of Chinese Biological Espionage': Source-The Week*)...took a hike, as they say, eh?

*It was as if...*we should listen to this lady (see: *'China's Missing Bat Woman Appears on TV, Says COVID-19 'Tip of the Iceberg': Source-outlookindia.com*), who reemerged linking the source

27

of *Novel Coronavirus* to animals, refuting outlandish conspiracy theories.

*It was as if*...the Military World Games were held in Wuhan, China in late October, '19, leading to numerous conspiracy theories, including the reported strange behavior of US athletes and the possible release of SARS-COV-2 (see: '2019 Military World Games: Source-Wikipedia)

*It was as if*...that munchkin activist from Sweden is the big winner here, as the carbon footprint is steadily shrinking (planes aren't dropping out of the sky, now...they're not taking off anymore)...

*It was as if*...Mass Media turned the 2020 US election into pandemic politics...why China wins again, ultimately.

*It was as if*...the Guv became the spy guy (see: 'NY Will Randomly Check Flight Passengers to Ensure They Quarantine': Source-Democrat and Chronicle), assuming an authoritarian throne.

*It was as if*...the politicians gave up on the 'Big Apple' (see: 'Weekly NYC Shootings Soar 358% Over Last Year, Data Shows': Source-NBC)

*It was as if*...Brains no longer mattered much (see: 'Fireworks Sales Skyrocket in US, Noise Complaints up Nearly 4,000% in NYC': Source-Business Insider)

*It was as if...BLM*

*It was as if...ALM*

*It was as if...GLM...on Mars!*     **The End**

## 'BEHIND CLOSED DOORS WITH THE BIG-LEAGUE BUNCH'

"They're really trying to destroy me, now. This is all a bunch of fucking bullshit!" the President shouted.

There was a brief hush, now, at the conference table. Cabinet members sat motionless expecting this sort of reaction, having just received another alarming briefing from China, of the rapidly spreading virus, of deteriorating conditions within their economic *boiler-room,* Wuhan, home to its own World Trade Center, expansive 5G networking, and ten million citizens.

His own *expansive* Secretary of State, a seemingly congenial, yet, hard-nosed and iron-fisted global mediator, Pompeii, got down to brass tacks, as they say.

"This is serious, Mr. President. We may need to take immediate action. Reports are coming in from…" He was cut off sharply.

"It's a HOAX!"

More silence. Sitting beside POTUS was his brilliant and beautiful daughter, and beside her, his porcelain statue son-in-law, an, altogether, prepossessing, dynamic and *dynastic* power couple, who danced a nifty tango, while turning the Emolument Clause on its daft head.

The family empire held well over a hundred patents, in China, to further their collective *brand*-spices and embroidered pillows, even-yet, the President maintained a combative stance, furthering his time-honored tradition as fierce negotiator and pugilist, while tossing all caution to the wind…only now, he had a global stage to perform on, with a shrewd and cunning adversary, China's Central

Government, forever poised like a charmed Cobra, and more than obliged to toss the gloves off and *throw down*, over the usual...Intellectual Property theft, outsourced jobs, the disputed South China Sea...and, now, a really searing brand, smoked in their hides, POTUS liked to call...the "Kung Flu".

"We aren't fucking China!" he roared, taking a momentary pause to let the words sink in for those seated about the impressive mahogany table. He turned his head back and forth, scanning the room. "And...if you think we're shutting this ship down, you are...WRONG!" His lips puckered as he said the word. Vanka drew in a deep breath, as her nattily attired hubby, Jarod, stared straight ahead, bumping knees.

"May I say something, Mr. President?" Corona Czar Fucci reluctantly asked. "I'm almost afraid to," he quipped in his trademark soft shoe style, relieving some tension. A few in the room even laughed. Antonio Fucci had served as health advisor to five previous administrations, was highly regarded in the field, and was married to Christina, the nation's Bioethics Czar…together, they were a human traffic light, wielding   influence over health policy, right or wrong.

"Go ahead" the President allowed, not smiling.

"This is something that could easily spiral out of control…this virus that is."

"It's not here," the President quickly responded.

"But it is," Fucci countered… "And, it's a crafty bugger…one that sneaks up without you knowing it. Look how China's handling it? Whole country locked down, taking preventative measures, in the most strident ways imaginable." He tried speaking in as plain English, as possible.

"We're not China," POTUS said flatly. "We're not CHINA, and we're not shutting DOWN," he reiterated, bitingly, blowing smoke rings with his lips.

The marble couple sat astride, stoned-faced, like 'Patience' and 'Fortitude', lion and lioness. Vanka bumped Jarod's knee back, smiling slightly, now. The slightness of it drew the attention of all males assembled, at once, as if she twerked their sensibilities, even before she spoke.

"Dad...ummm...Mr. Prez..."

"It's ok, Vanka...you don't have to hesitate..."

He flashed his broad smile and the table burst, in a spasm of laughter. She flashed back her own gorgeous, toothy smile, owning the moment. The Cabinet males shifted in their seats, reflexively, staring intently. The few women present wondered, dreamily, to themselves, how another of their gender could, possibly, be crafted of such physical perfection.

"Well, it's the election season after all, and whatever you do, you know the press is going to *cream* you," she exclaimed matter-of-factly. One stiff suit coughed, practically choking.

"We're not doing ANYTHING!" he repeated. "It's ALL fake news…right, Big Mike?"

He stiffened his back and crossed his arms, turning to the corpulent Secretary of State, seated to his immediate right, like a bodyguard.

"It's spreading like wildfire to Spain, Italy, France, like dominoes," the well-travelled Pompeii responded, flatly. "Even Iran."

"I hadn't heard that."

"Unfortunately, it's true, Mr. President…and we best be prepared here." Big Mike was a straight-shooter, when he needed to be.

"What about you, Pencer? What's your take?"

He could always count on the white-haired, trusty VP to take his side on a host of running issues, and soften the blow, especially, in media matters.

"How will this *work* with the Evangelicals…you know…our base? Or, the NASCAR crowd…you know…gun guys? We need them in our corner. We're going to _where_ next month? Manchester? We'll _dust_ them there."

"…and North Charleston, Mr. President," Secretary Wolff remarked.

"But, I thought we needed Suoth Carolina."

Vanka whispered in her father's ear.


"North Charleston is IN South Carolina, Dad."

He shrugged, frowning sheepishly, a bit.

The president continued to hold rallies, deep into February, continued reacting with absolute defiance, as millions poured back into the states from Europe and Asia, through jammed airports, and cruise ships.

"AMERICA WORKS…and will keep on working!!!" Donaldo roared to thunderous applause and shouting, from the crowd. "Make no mistake. Look at this economy, the markets!" he shrieked, grasping the podium tightly. "Wall Street off the charts. Unemployment at an all-time low. African American employment at an all-time high. Greatest economic turnaround in the history of our great country...greatest nation on the face of the earth!"

The President was floating in air, high over the swollen North Charleston crowd.  When the arena quieted, he half-joked.

"You know, they might have to build a bigger rock at Mount Rushmore!"

"We love you, South Carolina!"

"God Bless you...and God Bless America!"

The President beamed, triumphantly, as the MAGA crowd went nuts. Hats flew everywhere.

In the space of a few short months, however, the delicate *house of cards* all came tumbling down...down like a freight train on a shaky sky bridge, collapsing under its own weight...down like Goliath taking it to the throat...a viral curse...yet, the party rolled on, regardless, for a while (...as in the words... "We're not China")...you could take the *madness* out of March and Mardi Gras would put it right back in...ka-ching ka-ching...beads, boobs & booze. Spring Breakers, too!

...and the rest is, well...history.

**THE END**

# 'THE CHILDREN' (part one)

"I won't, I won't...and you can't make me!"

Carl sat in his easy chair, oblivious to the goings on around him. The television was turned off. Over and over he tossed his neatly stitched baseball lightly into the air, while staring at the blank screen in front of him. He was in a trance dreaming of box seats, the crack of the bat, the smell of wieners and popcorn, the deafening roar of the crowd...

"I won't EVER allow you to play Xbox with your little brother, Janie!"

Carla stood at the bottom of the stairs, waiting for her daughter's response.

"GOOD!"

The petulant little girl stood with her back braced against the locked bedroom door. Their dog Sparky barked away at a frenzied pace.

All across America, some families were beginning to lose their collective minds. The immutable, immoveable father didn't hear a thing in the middle of all this upheaval. It was early April, and the season was a long way from starting, if at all. He just sat numbly spinning his ball...over and over and over, again.

**THE END**

## 'THE CHILDREN' (part two)

"We'll wash your car, Mister!" one kid hollered, holding a hose, as their neighbor rolled around the residential cul-de-sac, in his spotless Mercedes.

"Dollar lemonade!" yelled another.

A cocker spaniel chased a calico cat that chased a red squirrel that scrambled up a tree. It was a sunny Monday morning, in late April, and everyone was at home, practically.  **THE END**

## 'PILING IN THE WELCOME WAGON'

The Clydesdale's piled into their wagon-well, not really-that would be an accelerated, *Flinstonian* back pedal spin, a not so timeless age, but, rather, one designed of a certain era-the 60's and 70's-when family trips, often involved a 'Country Squire', say, wood-panels and durable for the long haul...now, leaping ahead to mid-summer 2020, to be rather specific, and a long open road ahead on a *quest* (parents explaining to the youngsters they were embarking on a "pilgrimage", of sorts), inside a sleek minivan packed reasonably (as provisions lay await, pre-stocked), mainly of human cargo.

"Say so long to Pacific Palisades for now, kids!" Clarke Clydesdale chimed in an overtly cheerful manner, turning his head from the driver's perch for his taciturn crew piled in back. The two teens, Oswald and Minerva ignored him entirely, his daughter texting madly away, with her friends, while "Oz" engaged in endless laptop war games. Only pint-sized Philomena rose to her daddy's occasion, wide-eyed in his mirror, watching her leafy neighborhood pass by through the windshield portal. She sang out, "Goodbye, Mr. Gate", and they were gone from the community, at large.

"When should we expect to arrive, Clarke?" wife Constanza asked, feeling blindsided by the shimmering glare of Utah's Bonneville Salt Flats...like skimming over an endless moonscape. "This place is dizzying," she swooned. "Maybe, it's early menopause."

"Look, Daddy...it's a lake!" Philomena shrieked. Minerva gave her little sister a sharp elbow, and she yelped. "It's not a *lake,* dummy...it's called a mirage." Clarke just laughed. "Couple of days...give or take a couple of days," he responded, finally. "That tells me a lot," his wife groaned.

Clarke was in no rush, certainly, time being somehow limitless and unconstrained, under the circumstances. The second *lockdown* was a boomerang effect to the forehead. Production sets dark, at a standstill, industry ground to a halt, again. Looking at a few months, most likely, before 'Season Eight' could resume filming...again. Clarke directed a popular, weekly crime show.

The *virus*...or, whatever it was...didn't bode well for the so-called, *City of Angels,* at all. His head felt squeezed like a slow vice, by ALL the bad news, nation-wide...the incessant chatter and clatter of the airwaves, spewing out daily horrors of masked misery...of statistics, and protests, and senseless, sporadic spates of violence and hatred happening, all at once, seemingly....what was the next coming attraction, the *Big One?*...city cracking like an egg, swallowing them whole? <u>THAT</u> would be the *Perfect Storm,* alright. Time to get away.

"Where are we going, Daddy?" five year-old Philomena asked for the hundredth time. Clarke broke out in hysterical laughter.

"To the bunker, Phil…the bunker…the bunker…the bunker!"

"You are such a square, Dad," Minerva sniffed. "You're like having Clark Kent for a father…especially, with those black glasses. Aren't Hollywood director's supposed to be cool and wear shades, and get high and everything?" she cracked, sardonically. "I need a joint."

"That's enough young lady," her mother snapped. "There ARE impressionable minds riding along, you know…and, you know, maybe this is a good time to mention…the dour, *goth* look is so 90's, you think? Maybe, you could spruce up, a tad before we arrive?" Constanza *clicked* and winked, at once, in her daughter's direction, craning her neck a bit too quickly, in the process.

"And…just maybe, you could use a brow lift, *Kwanzaa*…as in *hut*? For the good old crow's feet, Ma? Sorry, trying to stay politically correct, ha!"

45

"Ok...ok, now. I know...we're all a bit testy from the long trip, but, let's try keeping the insults to a minimum." Clarke offered.

Her gaming-induced brother found this tat-for-tat a nice distraction from the endless miles, smiling slightly, without bothering to avert his eyes from his screen.

"What's a bunker, Daddy?" Philomena asked.

The van sped steadfastly along.

'Garden of the Gods'... 'Cornhuskers'

"A bunker is a figment of the imagination, *kitten,*" the congenial dad answered a few states later, after being asked a thousand times. Philomena was one bright light in his life, along with his loyal wife, of course. He loved them all, despite an assortment of flaws. No family was perfect, after all, and the Clydesdale's were no exception, certainly.

"C'mon, Clarke, explain to your daughter," his wife chided. *"Phil* won't stop asking until she gets a clear picture in her head where we're taking them."

"A bunker is a pile of dirt that you live in," Minerva wisecracked. "Very foreboding, inhospitable place, *Philly*......place you don't want to go."

"Minny!" her mother snapped. "Your little sister is too young to understand these things!"

"Well...I...want...to...go!" Philomena whooped, throwing her arms in the air, warming her daddy's heart.

"Oh, we're here! We're in the Black Hills," Clark stated, matter-of-factly. A long way from home. A yellow-jacketed security official, standing astride his idling ATV, waved them forward, and the minivan rolled down the ramp...a ramp not so dissimilar to any old underground parking garage, but, in this case, stuck in the middle of nowheresville.

"This is exciting!" Philomena yipped like a cougar cub. "This...sucks." Oswald groaned. Their casually-attired *Captain* dad steered his "ship" past a line of shiny, parked family-packs...Beemer's & Caddies...lots of dazzling sports cars, too...all late-model, of course. "Look-a Phantom!" Oz whooped. "Cool!"

'Welcome TO VIVOSSOX'

The mini-van rode under a large sign, lettered in battleship grey, and were waved forward, again, toward another ramp, where they ascended to the plains baked sprawl of retrofitted army munitions dumps. The kids were semi-awestruck by the sight, being more accustomed to coastlines and craggy cliffs, and gated communities, and skyscrapers, and endless freeways. Fortified concrete and steel mounds dotted an, otherwise, barren landscape stretching as far as the eye could see.

"What... is...this...place?" Minerva crowed.

"We're home!" Clarke intoned, stretching now and spreading his arms wide as if to embrace the moment, and the whole blasted scene. They may have well been marooned on the Red Planet.

"We're staying with the Parker's and the Silverton's", their mother added.

"The...WHO?" all three kids asked in unison.

The dark, virus cloud eventually passed, leaving behind a trail of tears and broken hearts across the land, coast to coast, a somewhat shattered economy for struggling masses (while the rich enriched themselves, craftily)...the Clydesdale's, meanwhile, weathered their own storm quite nicely, within the protected walls of their getaway...for an entire month!

Speaking of walls. Constanza gave up keeping track of her *spitfire* Philomena, who quickly turned the cubicle bunker into her own hide-and-seek playground. She and Alice Silverton traded spaces and places like interchangeable parts, zipping about like little *tomahawks,* whooping it up.

Oswald fell head over heels with doll-eyed Pauli Parker to the point his dad-resorting to a bit of awkward father-son intercession...well, that didn't work, clearly. The eighth-graders spent half the time making out. Fifteen heads, in all, squeezed into a doable living space, full of the amenities and provisions of modernity....home away from home, so to speak...clunky refrigerators spitting out ice spheres at a continuum...moody Minerva, relentlessly, pressing the quick flush toilets, in fits of annoyance. "People not Bombs" was, fittingly, spray painted on her own cubicle wall. Three families, with three kids apiece, and martinis for the adults.

They all made the best of it, and parted the best of friends, before piling back into their *welcome wagons* for the long trek home. The sky hadn't fallen in, after all!  **The End**

## 'GRETA'

There once was a girl from Sweden, who told millions of classmates she would need 'em
She cast a strange spell, to all she could tell, that all was not well.

The skies they soon cleared

The skies they soon cleared

The skies they soon cleared

She was further endeared

Dear Planet

# NUTBALLS...NUTWINGS...& DELIRIOUS THINGS

1- 'Silda Blows the Whistle on the Hairy White Ape'

2- 'Smoke n' Mirrors'

3- 'Kelly Ann, George, & Claudina'

4- 'The Debate Rages On-A Podcast'

5- 'A Gaffe A Minute, If You Can Believe It'

6- 'Clarabellina Hits the Deck'

7- 'Reflections on the Year That Wasn't'

## 'Silda Blows the Whistle on the Hairy White Ape'

Silda Clackhorn wanted to take a stand...a determined, defiant and dastardly one, for society's vile fringe to take notice-a wake up call, so to speak, for that...fringe, you say? Huh? The 'Equity, Diversity, and Inclusion' *club*?...some kind of twisted aberration to be accepted as an absolute, in the universal sense?...Gender dysphoria, nope!...not in Silda's mind. The various movements of kooks, crackpots, and gross oddities were no longer an exception to the rule, but the rule itself! Life was out of whack, and a distinct threat to her steely, yet diminishing, reserves of <u>tolerance</u>. She was running out of <u>that</u>, entirely...mainstream had been co-opted, overwhelmed, and hijacked by the radical left.

Silda's placid husband, Jacob, quietly turned the page of his morning paper, role-playing like Robert Young in 'Father's Knows Best', desiring nothing but *the usual* out of life...an unrumpled, crisp suit unblemished by lint, hair carefully parted on the side nicely trimmed, and spectacles free of grit.

"I won't stand for it!" cackled the bony-framed woman, her eyes ablaze with fury to make a rattler's skin crawl, borne of a womanhood linked, ancestrally, to pioneers of invigorating protest and upheaval, whether of Prohibition, Suffrage, or beyond, in the matriarchal sense. The women of her *tree* seemed all to have been tall, thin, and fiercely determined.

"Look at me, Jacob!"

Her husband calmly let his newspaper rest on the linoleum table, peering over his *Dalton Green's*, like Chuck Schumer, who he idolized.

"The *Blue Bunch* stink to high heaven!" Silda shrieked.

"They think MY child's going to sit in a room with some hairy freak of an ape man, dressed like a barbarian...like a *woman*...it's monstrous, and I'll tell those Neanderthal librarians just that!"

"Now, now, love," Jacob reflected earnestly, "Don't you think you're taking this a bit too far, this...this apparent obsession...harangue even? It's upsetting to young Jules here, I would venture to say."

Jules blinked rapidly, uncertain how to process his parents daily ritual, at breakfast. Strange, confusing chatter that made no sense to him. All the little boy knew was that his father never really seemed bothered much by his mother's incessant ravings. He had insurance work to do, after all, at the agency, and seemed completely disaffected by life, in general. He didn't go to ball games, like his co-workers, or play poker with drinking buddies, or, any of that. Normalcy was just that, which he desired above all, it seemed.

Impish Jules sank slowly in his chair chewing a piece of toast, which caught Silda's attention. He quickly sat up straight, offering his statuesque mother a sheepish grin.

"That's better, young man."

Jules was a bit too waifish, and reticent, in her estimation, but, that was probably a good thing. He'd find his strapping youth soon enough. He gave his mother a sheepish grin. She bent her long frame over and peered closely into her son's eyes, with mesmerising effect, then quickly snapped him back to attention.

"Now, run along and grab your coat and hat."

The boy shifted carefully in his seat, not averting her watchful eyes, and slinked quietly out of the kitchen.

"You do have a grip on that boy," Jacob acknowledged.

"Well, you're so absorbed by the bric-a-brac news print you devour with your oatmeal, every morning, to seem too concerned by ancillary trivialities...like child development, for instance."

Her husband ignored the slight. "He's only six, dear," Jacob dully rebuffed, dabbling his mouth

71

corners at nothing in particular. "I'm off to the trenches, my love. Go easy on those librarian's, please." She offered a wry smile back, but felt her throat tighten and a tinge of nervous anxiety at the mere mention of what she perceived to be an inevitable confrontation, with a willing adversary, in due time...the *adversarial* part being, exclusively, in her own mind, of course. Her husband thought of Silda as a bit of a *nutball,* if not an endearing one, at times. They were polar opposites, after all. Jacob favored the *Red Bunch*...donkey's to elephant's, say.

Pint-sized Jules looked skyward at his towering mother as she strode purposefully, practically swinging the boy in the library parking lot, like a kite ready to launch.

"Mom...I...can't...keep...up," he cried pleadingly. "You're hurting my arm!" he yelped.

"We're about there, son."

They both heard sounds, at a distance, from the library, it seemed, that that became louder and louder, as they drew closer. Raucous, unearthly sounds, it seemed. She steadied their pace, approaching with a note to herself of caution, not knowing what to expect. What WAS going on there, they both wondered?

"We're here son...here we are." Silda confirmed twice. They both stood in the open doorway of the crowded library, hand in hand, gazing upon a scene of merriment, of myriad radiant colors, of signs and banners and balloons and outlandish outfits, like a rainbow broken into numerous moving parts, of mothers and children, alike, dancing and swinging about a feathery maypole, frollicking, skipping and hopping about the room, accompanied strangely by the dizzying sounds of crazy carousel music emanating from wall speakers-Silda's least favorite sound in the world-that scene from 'Strangers on a Train' (she swore off Hitchcock after that). Silda cupped her hands over her ears and shook her orange-topped head sideways, back and forth, as if one ear was being pulled one way, then the other, by an unseen force...a feeling of vertigo. All little Jules could do was look up. What he saw was his mother in distress. Her eyes were squeezed shut.

He watched a larger, comical-looking boy, wearing a girl's skirt and blouse, pogo into a shelf of children's books, that crashed on top of him. This got Silda's attention. Her eyes opened to the chaotic scene as the carnival music came to an abrupt stop. Library ladies, dressed for the occasion, in wigs and clownish apparel, rushed over to assist the sprawled out boy-in-a-skirt, slapping at the fallen books covering his big head. It was this moment that the statuesque Silda noticed something squirming in the furthest corner of the quieted room. She shook her head, in disbelief. Two children were squirming...no, straddled ...upon a much larger body...a mammoth *thing* stretched flat on its back. Her eyes hurt and ears rung...*sensory overload*...she struggled to maintain a grip and focus but was quickly catapulted into the

74

phantasmagoric horror of horrors of a scene, of a deranged man staring in space at the ceiling, flat on his back, a twisted frozen smile on his mascara-streaked face, like a dead clown...his tree-trunk hairy legs and crotch were exposed and a sickly dress billowed about his chest. A little boy and girl were wrapped around his torso, spread-eagled, hugging him. Silda gasped when she realized the transvestite was in a state of sheer bliss.

"Mom, that *girl*...that MAN is only wearing underwear!" Jules cried out in astonishment..

"Look away, son...cover your eyes."

Silda had, suddenly, snapped into razor-sharp attention, like she had been zapped by lightning. She had, after all, prepared herself for a moment like this. She unclasped her purse and reached for the silvery object in one fluid motion.

Jules didn't recognize it, at first, but it had been a stocking stuffer treasure to go with the referee pajamas he wore a few Christmases past. Silda had called him her little *zebra*, then, as he raced around the ornamental tree yelling *"illegal motion on the offense"* and *"unsportsmanlike conduct on the defense"*...an uncanny ability at word retention for a child of four, his parents thought at the time...they wondered if the boy was "gifted", or, just plain autistic, but, that wasn't the case, thank goodness.

He watched his mother place the object to her lips. Her eyes were as wide as saucers. She scanned the room that appeared, now, as a jumble of the strange and sordid, and blew the shrill whistle mightily. All movement ceased, and all heads turned toward Silda, standing straight and tall as a tree, blowing like a keystone cop at a union strike riot.

The freakish blob in the corner continued staring into space, immoveable. The kids jumped off him real quick. 'Drag Queen Story Hour' was, officially, OVER!

**THE END**

## 'Smoke n' Mirrors'

Surname: (fictitious)

Maung-Burmese

Khatun-Bangladeshi

Kasongo-Congolese

Need grass? Dial up Ehud Ackermann's joint...now, that's the quality sh*t and not the half-assed, cheap crap of yesteryear, he was known for dispensing. In keeping with the times. You might expect a jeweller, or dentist, or house flipper with a name like that, but he's actually, a crafty artisan, and capable green thumb, and has lived with his doughy sister his whole life, it seems. Their elderly housebound mother finally passed, relieving the two of that caretaking duty, leaving them a comfortable, nondescript city domicile to share space and haggle over daily doings, and such.

Ehud's in his sixties, now...a bit of a *nutwing* (aren't we all?)...a tad cartoonish, in appearance, likes to laugh...an altogether wily, wry, wiry little guy who'll break into his best brown belt Bruce Lee stance, in a flash, and ninja voice...hoy-yaa!!!...loves the 'Giants'... 'The Stones'...oh yeah, and the staunchest of Democrat's in an upstate *sanctuary* town, famous for its "machine"...he'll stammer and shriek vociferously when triggered... "Republicans are all Nazi's"... "those horrible fascists"...that sort of thing...I don't believe it myself, whatsoever, but, to each his own.

I'm there at his *beck and call*, so to speak, hardly the other way 'round... "they just want to screw you, screw the worker, screw the maid, take it all for themselves". Yeah, ok.

Sinewy chap Ehud is, valiantly fought off some serious health scares, enlivened and reinvigorated with a fresh outlook...stream of consciousness sort of fellow...needs a woman (don't we all, huh), divulged a bit of electoral gamesmanship,

78

recently...Hmmm. Nothing unusual, really, in this town...lots of free thinkers. Ballot hauls and door-to-door *palling around* with some recent arrivals, say, the usual.

Freewheeling it in a precedent setting town, so to speak.

Is the "harvest" in...of the balloting kind? Hope this year beats the last stinker. Got a new "kid" on the big block, again...on the big stage...kind of a relic of the past nobody ever cared for much, ...wonder how he got there? Nobody seems to care much, as long as the other guy's gone...you know, the guy that never seemed to lose...until now, that is. Taking his beautiful, brilliant daughter with him. I'm sad about that. I wrote a short story about them in my last book, called 'Behind Closed Doors With the Big League Bunch' (July '20). It's kind of a hoot. Hope you'll read it some time soon (if i ever get around to publishing...my "stuff" seems to sit around a LOT gathering dust). I edited the crap out of this story, btw, why I'm flying off on a tangent, now. It's 3:37am and MLK, Jr Day has passed us by. Goodnight. **The End**

## 'Kelly Ann, George & Claudina'

Kelly Ann Connelly has always strived for success.

Her bloodline covers a lot of terrain-German, English, Irish, Italian-had a mobster grandfather called 'Jimmy th *pundettes*, who fit in perfectly with Team 'Donaldo', as Senior Counselor to the President. A constant presence in front of the cameras Kelly Ann was, undeniably, a  polished, sharp-witted, and unapologetic force to reckon with (regardless of your political leanings, really), not the least dissimilar to the whole Fox line-up of fierce, brilliant and blondish media savvy types, over the years...like Ann, Laura, Megyn, etc...(again, undeniable...love 'em or hate 'em). WH Press Secretary Kayleigh...AGAIN, fitting like a glove in the tough as nails 'Donaldo' camp. Makes the other team's cast of overweight media squawkers, sitting on panels looking like your morning's jelly-filled donut, seem kind of pathetic, you know? But, that's besides the point, because that's not what this is about. This is about family dysfunction, on an epic scale...and now, back to my original tale, prior to becoming lost in this edit...to half the country, Kelly Ann has the appeal of a stack of blueberry containers lined up in a row at your local supermarket, always seeming to grab your attention, not so much in the aromatic sense but, in sight alone, when you think about it...so, it's only fitting that President Donaldo's sharply focused and capable Senior Counselor was once crowned 'World Champion Blueberry Picking Competition' champion. Call her a crazy New Jersey girl, or not, and she'll tell you, "Everything I learned about life and business started on that farm." Eight hot summers in the fields is a LOT of picking!

"Hey Mom...guess what? Dad *dipped* and he's not coming back...thanks a lot!...did you see my latest Tik Tok count?"

The beleaguered teen's mom was accustomed to Claudina's tempers and tantrums, and the whole world was, too...another Generation Z superstar.

Kelly Ann gave her, oft, snotty daughter a quick glance before continuing to chop away at a stubborn thick pineapple. She then placed the knife gently on her juicy cutting board, before wiping her hands on her apron. Then she spoke.

"Don't you have anything better to do, young lady, then to stand there looking grievous and unforgiving? You seem to have become, practically, *subhuman* in your treatment of others. If you haven't forgotten as yet, I gave up a <u>White</u> <u>House</u> job, in an entirely vain attempt, it appears, to not only shore up my relationship with your contentious father, but to mend fences with my precocious sixteen year-old daughter. Look, Claudina. You're too young to have such a dispassionate, callous outlook on life...you, seriously, need an attitude adjustment, I think."

"Seriously, mom. Why did you and *George* get married? I mean, it's embarrassing, you two are like the Carville's...a mismatch." Claudina giggled in her mother's face.

"Do not call your father by his first name! It's...it's...*untoward*."

Kelly Ann was visibly upset, so the young sprite went for the jugular.

"Un-too-WHAT?" Claudina snapped. She tossed her head back, shaking her blonde locks, laughing uproariously, like someone possessed. She stopped suddenly, looking all serious. "You think I'm a witch, don't you mom?" and resumed her cackle. "I mean, it's a bit *presumptuous...preposterous*, even, don't you think, in this day and age, to use words like that? You know, we're not in the Victorian Age...a bit too *antiquarian*, if you ask me?" Claudina cocked her head and made a funny face, biting off some impressive

84

*Cockney*. Her mother couldn't help but laugh, a bit, and softened. She had a smart cookie for a daughter.

"You know what, young lady? I wasn't always such an old doddering fool. I wasn't much older than yourself when I graduated Magna Cum Laude, followed by an Oxford internship, before taking DC by storm. I've always been at the top of my game, and it's not an easy thing...life, I mean. You have too many brains to *just be* a media star. I'm no different than any other concerned parent who loves her child, and I always want the best for you...as your

Claudina wasn't exactly letting her mother off the hook that easily, 'tho, placing blame for her dad's exit. "There you go again, *Mommie Dearest*, Talking like an old fuddy duddy."

Kelly Ann flashed her best combative smile, one trained for the cameras in heated debates. She reached for her carving knife and returned to hacking her pineapple.

"Well, run along if you must..." Kelly Ann muttered.

...and crawl back to your *web*. You seem preeminently qualified, dishing out your family's dirty laundry to the globe...a habit it's become of persistent embarrassments, to keep your fans enthralled. Maybe one day you'll realize I always look out after your own best interests, dear. Is why we're born with a heart, don't forget, *Miss Goldilocks.* Go now...leave your mother in peace, please....and I love you, don't forget.

Claudina jerked around and strode defiantly out of the spacious kitchen toward their spiraling staircase. She could not believe, however, all things considered, how wonderful her mom was, actually.

"I love you, too, mom!" Claudina yelled.

**THE END**

## 'The Debate Rages On-A Podcast'

*"Essentially the Democrat Party serves militarism, imperialism, and corporatism...why you see neocons...you see Bush and Cheney operatives cheering for Joe Biden, why Wall Street celebrated when he picked Kamala Harris."*

-Glenn Greenwald

Moderator-Mort Lindell

From the Left-Adley Levi

From the Right-Bo Whitehall

"Good evening viewers and listeners, near and far across this great land of ours. My name is Mort Lindell, host of the weekly podcast, 'The Debate Rages On', and your "unfair and unbalanced" moderator for tonight's broadcast...ha ha... (lite laff track, minor applause). Just ask my wife-kidding! (bigger laffs-enthusiastic applause).

Tonight we have two special guests, one decidedly from the left, and one from the right...otherwise, what's the point, right? (laffs). Adley Levi is national political correspondent for the 'Times' and political science graduate of Columbia University (light applause). Bo Whitehall, on the other hand, is a babbling right-wing nutcase from Topeka, ha ha!...just kidding, folks! (big laffs). He's the erudite *amateur* guy you turn to for those feeling betrayed and begrudged by the *drudgery* of today's propagandist's (resounding boos). So let's take the gloves off...and remember, I'm not THAT 'Pillow' guy, 'tho we do share a last name!" (roaring laffs)...

Mort Moderator: We'll start with you Adley. It's Inauguration Day. A relic of the past, retread of a failed administration, has been resurrected from the dead in a highly questionable, and legally challenged election cycle. However, it's a done deal, now, and time to move on. How, Mr. Levi, have we fallen off the proverbial cliff, seemingly, from being that shining beacon on the hill, of unfettered free speech and open debate to a nation suffocating under the crushing weight of censorship, cancel culture and identity politicking...predominantly, a feature of today's virtue-signaling keeper's of the *diversity* flame...the Democrat Party (murmurs)...seems a tad contradictory.

Adley Levi. Are you sure he's *really* been resurrected, Mort? (nervous laffs). Look, for me, the job *was* a fat paycheck. I sold out long ago to stay in the game and stay <u>relevant</u>. My colleagues are no different. It's that word "relevancy". Trump made EVERYONE who was ANYONE...the Michael Moore's & Ralph Nader's & Robert Reich's of the world, totally irrelevant...along with ALL *Blue check* Hollywood, less than irrelevant, in Donald's world....the has-been hangers-on...Baldwin, DeNiro, Clooney...not to mention all liberal media. Trump called it for what it is...Fake News. Garbage culture. He was the most despised President of the modern-age, by far.

Mort Lindell: Well, I must say, I'm a bit confused and surprised to hear youuuu...

Adley Levi: I resigned today from the '*Xinhua Times*', actually, ha!...(audience gasp). I figure it's an abdication of journalistic integrity, of our responsibility as stewards of a *free press* NOT to become State-run media, which is what's happened. Beijing's rolling on the floor watching our neophyte stumblings, while kind of impressed at the same time, at the rapidity of our transformation. Hundreds of years of growth tossed out with the bathwater, so to speak, regressively-speaking. Russia is correct when they call our two-party system "archaic". China rules from a position of strength and what does our slap-happy meat grinder roll out? A weepy carcass of a leader who can't decide in the morning what right shoe to put on the wrong foot. RT is absolutely shredding us, making a mockery. They have the best contributing writers out there. Chris Hedges, for one. The Times Op-ed section, on the other hand, is 100% slanted left, including letters to the editor's. There is zero wriggle room for dissent, or opposing viewpoints. 'Arts & Leisure' is still half-believable, and how could it not be? (groans). Otherwise, we've become the CCP, media-wise...ALL LIBERAL MEDIA WISE. It's a tragedy few citizen's can really comprehend, but hardly an overnight development. This feckless, "queer" press ignored any Hunter story, of course, until AFTER the election. He globe-trobbed, smoked crack and who knows what else. Why do you think the Capitol was stormed? You think they're all dumb, racist red-necks? Tucker? Jimmy Dore?...last line of defense, swimming against the giant blue wave.

L Lin Wood the Q Anon attorney...speaking of. The 'Times' refers to child trafficking a "hoax", really? On the heels of Jeffrey Epstein? Mainly bored lefty elites-the immorals- who go younger and younger, big mystery. No telling the extent of their ritualist perversions. Look at pedo-island flight logs. Sidney Powell didn't abandon Trump...Senator's Josh Hawley, Ted Cruz, Marjorie Taylor Greene...heroes if you ask me. What's been the across-the-board media narrative since the election?...*no evidence of election fraud...baseless allegations...unsubstantiated claims...*despite reams of evidence to the contrary! A giant mail-in fraud it was, massive Biden dumps, obstructionism. The Judges wanted Trump gone, as well, forget the legal mumbo-jumbo. L Wood said it best, "Nobody loses 0-60 unless the deck is stacked."

Candace Owens is the independent-thinking Conservative African-American wonderkind who said it best, that the moment Democrat's initiated "lockdown", in early '20, the economic crash, in other words ...meaning Governor's and Mayor's of Blue cities...that the fix was in and her hero Trump would lose. He knew it as well, and I thought the same, for months and months...and guess what? This is hardly a *one and done*. The days of pulling levers behind the magic curtain? Gone, most like. Mail-in balloting at that epic scale is never to be trusted. Anyhow...

Mort Lindell: How did we get to this place, Bo?

Bo Whitehall: To quote Winston Churchill: *The empires of the future are the empires of the mind*. We've, collectively, lost ours.

Mort Lindell: The left calls the right fascist.

Bo Whitehall: I see it the other way around. The parties have flipped. Who spearheaded eight-years of war, in seven countries, preceding Trump? Who deported twice as many immigrants as Trump, and built the cages? Who ran guns to Mexican cartels, busted whistleblower's, spied on citizens, bailed out crooked banks? Who is still adored by liberal media? Today's Inauguration is a "*reward for failure*", in my opinion, but the voters are clueless, and don't care about drowning babies and grandmothers, apparently, sinking on crowded lifeboats in the Meditteranean, fleeing Libya. They'd rather watch 'Sanford & Sons' reruns...CNN...speaking of...five years of relentless Trump bashing, *progressively* lowering the dim switch of a "free press"...you know, *Evil Overlord* of a comic strip, with wind up anchor puppets, Comos & Homos, sorry...bad visuals *looping*...clowns, really, waste of talent. Unwatchable sh\*t...NBC, ABC, CBS, all one-sided. NPR on your radio dial. Unlistenable, silly stuff for lemonheads. Remember Phil Hendrie? THAT was radio! What does the average Biden voter know? That Blinken Tanden & Nuland is a law firm in Wisconsin, ha! They think a *cabinet* is where you store *non-perishable* items...like the *dinosaurs* who steer this ship. Bamboozled by *multiracial whiteness* and *manufactured consent?* Where's *Socrates* when we need him?...convicted of *impiety* and forced to drink hemlock, for defying the *gods of the state*, the Greeks. Democrats are choking the life out of our system. It's a tricameral stranglehold, now. They call any form of dissent *domestic terrorism*, if you can believe it.

That's not a slippery slope, that's an avalanche of trouble, in a sprawled out, heavily-armed country, such as ours.

I watch Jimmy Dore, Tucker...Bongino, even...anything to avoid the liberal bubble, and keep my sanity...Lionel Nation and his scattershot stream-of-conscious banter. I used to dial him up, in his syndicated days. Ever listen to Sergei Lavrov? Smart. He tells it like it is, from a foreign-policy standpoint, anyway. So did Iran's Ahmadinejad, if I recall. It became an annual tradition at the UN, calling out hypocrisy. Trump was a revolutionary figure the establishment could never reign in, and had to go...an apolitical *Reality Show* wildcat, turned dethroned king, so to speak. Toughest campaigner I've ever seen, by far.

That final weekend swing was one for the ages, tens of thousands standing out in freezing rain, for hours and hours, from Omaha to Topeka...Vegas, Greenville...the elderly, too. Biden's drive-in events an exercise in mockery. The fix was in, and Trump knew it...anyone with half-a-brain sensed it...the DNC orchestrated it. Heartbreaking and unconstitutional.

Mort Lindell: Censorship?

Bo Whitehall: It's alive and well, and here to stay. Indefinitely, I'm afraid. I've said it before, we make North Korea look good, at this point, in terms of our mainstream media.

Mort Lindell: Final thoughts on this Inauguration evening, Adley? JT & J Lo? Usual suspects? Ugly 'Handmaid's Tale' costumes & Gaga's *Mockingjay Pin*?...the real news?

Adley Levi: Now, that's some talent I had to miss, ha! You know, after I quit the paper, I watched an interesting Marx Brothers documentary, and skipped the speech. Chico was a life-long gambler, it turns out.

Mort Lindell: Hey, you learn something every day!...and that's the wrap, unfortunately (loud cheers and claps)...*like sands of the hour glass*. My thanks to

Adley Levi as he departs 'The Times', I have no doubt ...and Bo Whitehall, for some straightforward analysis of the day. Keep *flogging*......I mean, *blogging* it, pal. Not exactly a *raging* debate, at all,

it turns out...but, hey...not a complete waste of time, either! I'm your host Mort Lindell...& remember...not the 'Pillow' guy. Goodnight.  **The End**

## 'A Gaffe A Minute, If You Can Believe It'

*"This is the craziest race. I am running against the worst candidate in the history of Presidential politics and if I lose, it is more pressure. I wish he was good. I would have less pressure. How do you lose to a guy like that?"*

*-Donald J. Trump*

"What did he say?"

"I don't know.

"That's funny."

"No, it's not-doesn't make sense."

"I can't believe this sh*t. He's gonna be the next...WHAT?"

Presidential candidate Joe Biden showed up on Election Day, November 3rd, 2020, in a residential neighborhood in Philadelphia. It was a grey afternoon, and a smallish crowd stood assembled watching him, some occupying space on tenement steps even. Candidate Joe held up a megaphone and this is what he said:

"I want to introduce you to my grand...two of my granddaughters..." (places arms around granddaughter Finnegan Biden)... "This is my son, Beau Biden, who a lot of you helped elect to the Senate in Delaware. This is my granddaughter Natalie (crowd cheers)...Oh no, wait. I got the wrong one. This is Beau's daughter, and we're out campaigning together. And then Hunter's number two, who goes to school here in Philly...this is my granddaughter Finnegan."

One inner-city girl turned to another on their steps...

"Wait, he just said she was Beau... 'aint he the dead one?

"He gots the wrong granddaughter, he did. When he puts his arm around the one...now, he gots the right one, I think." She smacked her hands on her large thighs, laughing uproariously, as heads turned in her direction. "This shit's too funny," another in the group said. "And people cheering him?...they stoopit, I think...dat's dumb...I wouldn't vote for THAT guy!" The girls laughed. Their astute friend didn't think it was funny, at all. She felt downcast, disappointed, staring straight ahead, as if in disbelief. She knew the son Beau had never served in the Senate, either.

America was about to elect half-a-nutcase to lead the world (as the *nuclear football* tags along)...a strangely controlling one, with a predilection, over the years, for (openly) flirting...ogling...groping...and sniffing little girls at Senate chamber photo op's...some as young as five, or, so...stroking their hair, creepily even, as their parents looked on nervous-like, uncertain how to react...and, now, liberal media ignored the GAFFE OF ALL GAFFES OF ALL TIME...on Election Day, no less! Foreign press were all over it, from India, China, Russia and England. 'Fox', too, of course...'Breitbart'...bellwether's of the Conservative cause.

Gaffe-a-minute Biden had become a sad running joke displayed at Trump rallies, on Jumbotrons. "Roll the tape", Donald would say, somewhat wearily, knowing he was destined to lose, despite the big, boisterous crowds...knowing he couldn't overcome the mail-in balloting bs. The *Beau* thing has won more elections for *Creepy Joe* than any other tool in his box...the sympathy factor, that is. He simply had to squeeze IT in one last time, no matter what, screwball as it sounded. Maybe, I reflected, in hindsight, it wasn't a gaffe at all. That, alone, is the strangest of thoughts. Delirious, really.

**The End**

### 'Clarabellina Hits the Deck'

"Get off me you pig!" Clarabellina squealed with delight as the coiffed stud drove into *her* hard. "You smell like cheap whiskey."

*Horse* flopped on his back breathing heavily.

"I swear you were the *Queen of Versaille* but this peacock's got to fan his feathers for an early morning engagement...and you've got to GO, DOG!...now be an angel and run along...OH MY!!!" *She* waved him away.

Horse hitched up his tight jeans, tossed a few bills on Clarabellina's night stand, lost his balance, momentarily, then stole a glance in *her* prized Fifi mirror, before disappearing into the night.

The next morning Clarabellina felt like an anvil had dropped on her head. *She* tossed *whatever* on, smeared her face with colorful junk and looked like a human train wreck. While *her* engine idled in the driveway, *she* reached for a matted wig on the floor of *her* front seat, and mashed it on *her* head.

She frowned at herself in the rear-view mirror, channeling her best inner tragic clown, then broke out in maniacal cackles. "Perfect!!!" *she* exclaimed to herself. "I'll scare the crap out of the little snots, and piss off the *500 Mums*, all at once!...and better yet...get paid!"

*She* coughed hoarsely then, after spasms of laughter. "Ok Ok, time to regain some composure, Clarallina." *She* took a few deep breaths before driving off in the direction of the Michelle Obama Library.

The mother-daughter founders of Spokane's *500 Mums* activist group were interviewed by the local Long Beach news the previous night. They had made the trip in support of concerned mothers who planned to protest the event being held, and Clarabellina, the featured attraction, happened to catch the interview on *her* flat screen as *she* channel surfed, munching on popcorn. The *transphobic* ladies were a slight nuisance to *her*, unworthy of any homicidal ideation she may have secretly coveted, in weightier matters...like some of *her* troublesome *tricks*, for instance. These clumps of, otherwise, *heteronormative* agitator's were just that...a source of agitation to the routine, like passing by a pack of barking dogs, huddled together on a sidewalk.

Clarabellina felt the full range of capricious emotions on the way to the library. Hangovers affected *her* in strange, unpredictable ways, often. *She* could feel laden down by self-loathing and disgust one minute, then cheerful like Audrey Hepburn the next, like dark clouds zapped by the sun's rays, in May. *She* could "shift those gears" she called it, at the sound of a car horn honking, or a friendly wave from an unfamiliar motorist sitting at a red light.

After squeezing *her* '78 LeBaron hurriedly into a tight space in the library parking lot, Clarabellina, suddenly, felt light as a feather stepping out of the vehicle...demurely coquettish even, as she thought of 'Horse' the night before. He had treated her brutally. *She* strode purposefully past the howling placard-waving primadonna bunch, through a wedge formed by library security; a floating sensation it was, as if *she* was the Fairy Godmother, parting the Red Sea. The crowd's anger was palpable, regardless. They held signs that read 'No Indoctrination'... 'Don't Groom My Child'... 'Freak Go Home'. They were horrified by the sight of *her*.

Clarabellina didn't notice, at all. *Her* tall frame hesitated before the sliding doors, before stepping inside. *She* felt like Bathsheba at home in her kingdom, now. Unruly children clamored about the festively festooned room, then quickly settled on the floor in a semi-circle, obediently (like kittens awaiting a slaughter, ha!)...an exuberant and expectant rainbow tribe they all were-of WOKE mom's and their little *charges.*

Marjorie, meanwhile, blended in, seamlessly, with the crowd (or so she thought), snapping pictures to be posted on social media, soon enough. *She* was the mum's "plant", yet no one seemed to care, although the colorfully dressed librarian's kept a wary eye on her.

'Drag Queen Story Hour' was very much a national thing, and part of the gravest kind of militancy, in the mum's minds...of *fringe* gone mainstream...a movement described as "grotesque mockery of femininity"...of "grown men dressed as sexualized clowns, adherents to religion called Queer Theory"...a *caliphate* of the worst imaginable connotation of the word. The notion of subjecting little children to this culture, of *gender fluidity*, as '*Radar*' called it (a gross term, by itself, really), was abhorrent to the mum's sensibilities, and they appeared, in pockets of protests, at every ALA-sponsored library event ...events their "Activist Mommy" leader compared to the dehumanizing *black-face* minstrel shows of the 19th Century, where '*Little Black Sambo*' came to be known.

Clarabellina shifted uncomfortably on her bottom, holding the book 'Julian is a Mermaid' upside down. *She* wished to be as close to the little riveted children as possible, but the floor wasn't working out so well, at the moment. The combination of bright lights, color and a million pairs of eyes became dizzying, and *her* empty stomach groaned with extreme displeasure. Just then a wave of nausea overcame her, like a red tide, and Clarabellina swooned... "I don't feel sooooo..." Her apt pupils cocked their heads, staring straight ahead, transfixed on their faltering *subject*, as doting mother's stood under an emblazoned banner in the background, confused by the unfolding drama, giving each other uncomfortable looks.

"I think I'll just...lay...down" Clarabellina stammered, as *her* 6'3'frame fell straight back, *hitting the deck*, as they say, with a giant thud...like a ton of bricks succumbing to a sledgehammer's blow. A pair of hypervigilant five-year olds quickly pounced on top of her, a boy and a girl, and the librarians leapt into action. "Children...NOOoooooooooo!!!

Late arrivals, Silda and Jules stood in the doorway, mother and son. It looked like the circus and the storm. The librarian's were busy removing books off a child's head, it appeared. Two kids were crawling on some hulking figure laid prone on the floor. Suddenly a shrill whistle pierced the air, and all movement momentarily ceased. The two kids leapt off the enormous frozen frame, like pronking gazelles. Silda smiled, her little boy shrugged and together they skipped merrily away from the building, holding each other's hands tightly. The nightmare was over.  **The End**

'Reflections on the Year That Wasn't...An Op-Ed'

*"First and foremost, I think I have been the only Republican conservative that has been calling out the rigging of this election since February. The second that Democrats started talking about these lockdowns, the second that America went <u>into</u> a lockdown, the fix was in. This is the greatest rigging of an American election that has ever taken place."* - *Candace Owens*

*"This election was the most watched, and perhaps for that reason, the cleanest election I think we've seen in American political history." -Rick Hasen CNN Election Law Analyst*

In divided America, with political chasms wider than the Grand Canyon, these two diametrically opposed quotes tell the tale of a nation falling off a cliff.

April 25th, 2019 was, arguably, the lowest point in American electoral history, in my mind, anyway...the day Joe Biden entered the 2020 Presidential race. Why? Because, like Candace, I, instinctively, knew he could win. I went audible, standing alone in my apartment watching the news that day... "Ohhh, Noooooo!". Where were YOU when you heard the news that fateful day, I wonder?

A stranger I met once, off-handedly, said it best, probably, that he had never met anyone who really <u>did</u> like Joe, actually!...or, had any <u>real</u> thoughts about him. That sums it up, nicely. But *Tough Guy* Joe has stuck around, like an infected toe, you know, with a treasure trove of unseeming, social *gropes* and *gaffes* and *falsehoods* and *policy blunders* to catapult to the top of the heap of a planet's spiralling-out-of-control global dysfunction. In other words, if we're truly experiencing the end of 'Empire', as many see it, wouldn't it be the face and character of a guy like Joe to usher in that inevitable collapse...like the poster child of ALL things going terribly wrong? Think of the stamina involved in running the world? The only question that remains, really, is when does he, ultimately, burn out and the DNC hand the reins over to Kamala? Embarrassing reality. In fact, to drive the point home, in a nutshell, if there's ever been a more notorious public figure, or, *candidate,* better-suited for spending some waning time casting a bobber out of a drowsy rowboat on a lazy pond, who, can you imagine, would that be?

January 1st, 2020 was a memorable day, the day 'Bail Reform 19' took effect in New York State. Any reasonable, non-partisan half-wit had to think it was some really bad April Fool's joke passed on that day, in 2019. Had the tricameral Democrat-run legislature lost its collective mind, or, was it just a three-headed dragon appeasing its downstate demographics, and the ACLU lobby?

'Bail Reform 19' had zero support from any law enforcement (quite the opposite) throughout the state, and placed the entire citizenry at the mercy of empowered violent criminals. It involved 155 crimes, in all, stripped judges of any discretion, and further forced innocent crime victims to instantly divulge personal information to defense attorney's, like phone numbers and addresses-passed, deceptively, in the colorful language of "non-violent" crime. The worst bill ever passed by New York State, in other words, and an absolute betrayal to its people. The results of this clunk-headed exercise in insanity, was foreboding and predictable. By the middle of the year, shooting and homicides had nearly tripled throughout the state.

Governor Cuomo, or 'King Andrew' had some other surprises up his sleeve, in 2020. Shipping Covid patients to nursing homes, with foreseeable results. Over ten-thousand died, prematurely, with a cover-up subplot, to make matters worse. When the positivity rate sunk below 1%, for months at a time, he kept the state *locked down* indefinitely. Other Blue State Governor's quickly followed suit, assuring a crashed national economy and a despised President's ultimate defeat...liberal media was the Governor's *bitch* and an eagerly compliant one at that...<u>he won an Emmy!</u>

Trump, meanwhile, read the tea leaves, to wit: *"The lamestream media is the dominant force in trying to get me to keep our country closed as long as possible, in the hope that it will be detrimental to my election success."* He saw the writing on the wall.

(see: 'Great Reset'...'Transforming Our World-The 2030 UN Agenda for Sustainable Development'/ 'Event 201-A Pandemic Exercise to Illustrate Preparedness') ('Governor Cuomo Signs the New York State on 'PAUSE' Executive Order, March 20, 2020('Trump Charges Media Wants Businesses Closed to Defeat Him'...March 25, 2020) (**'Media Ignore Hunter Biden Ties to China'**)

**I had to sneak that one in**...a sordid true-life adventure of family corruption, dating to 2013...and the reality of an all-consuming, complicit, censoring media.

*"Ten days after they (VP Joe & Son) returned from the (China) trip, Hunter Biden's small, private equity firm, called Rosemont Seneca Partners, gets a $1 billion private equity deal with the Chinese government."*

So, there you have it...censorship has not only taken root, in the land of the *free* and home of the *brave*, but is conjoined at the hip with One-Party Rule, now.

It's the biggest story of the whole year, in an awful, ruinous way, the end of the American dream! Any dissent is painted with a broad brush, into the ugliest painting imaginable. It made me sad seeing a photo of the tearful First Daughter and Senior Policy Advisor, Ivanka, as the First Family prepared to fly out of Andrews AFB for the Sunshine State, one last time, Inauguration morning. Her dad was making one final speech, as Commander-In-Chief. I'll miss Kayleigh, as well, the devout, sharp-as-a-whip Harvard Law grad White House Press Spokesperson. No sooner had she landed in Florida, the media shutterbug vultures pounced, posting *citizen* Kayleigh making the rounds, sans make-up. Public shaming? An unflattering look? The woman had a preventative double-mastectomy, at age thirty! She has God in her heart, which beats all! First Lady Melania was a trip, too, gracious and well-spoken, and despised by the liberal press (reason enough to like her, ha!). As for the 'Donald', I never watched the 'Apprentice', because I never liked the guy...and he turned out to be my favorite President! At least in a PT Barnum way.

The biggest revelatory moment of the year, I thought?

Realizing that Jesus walked the earth at the same time many of today's Sequoia's were taking root! In other words...the 'Tree of Life' lives! Blessings in His name.

*"Men and brethren, children of the stock of Abraham, and whosoever among you feareth God, to you is the word of this salvation sent."* Amen

(Bible Verse-Acts 13:26-27 Quote by Jimmy Carter

Victoria Advocate)

## 'Alexandria & Leopold-A Survivor's Tale'

Little ten-year old Alexandria desperately hung on to the upper reaches of a backyard Mango branch, as angry hurricane gusts ripped and roared through their demolished neighborhood. Her big brother, Leopold, eleven, kept a fierce grip on his own, next to her, blinking in rapid succession, as sheets of salty rain stung his eyes and pelted his body, relentlessly, watching intently as trees and shrubs and cottage shingles and dining room chairs flew by, as if spun by a terrific tornado.

All was lost, save for the blurred vision of spectral light dancing in the nighttime sky, sweeping the tumultuous coastline...light from the Cabo Rojo Lighthouse, easily recognizable to the kids, in calmer times, but now, truly, their one beacon of hope, if only in a purely ghastly way.

"Ayuadame, por favor !!!", Alexandria screamed.

"Help us! Helpppppp !!!!!!!", Leopold yelped.

The children swung with the tree, and as it snapped, flinging the pair like a double-barreled slingshot into another wild gust, all time stopped, and for a moment, they felt suspended, in mid-air...arms outstretched, fingers reaching for the stars...AND, just then, like an answered prayer, appeared a giant, winged albatross, clutching the siblings in its massive talons, carrying them high over the menacing clouds, away from the horrible storm, into the virtual unknown.

# Chapter One

'Snow Leopard'

Himalayan Mountains in a blizzard. The children, Alexandria and Leopold are mountain climbing. They have ropes and gear for the ascent up a massive cliff and stop for a breath along a ledge, just below the craggy peak.

"Que es eso, Leo?", the small girl asked her brother, pointing to another ledge nearby, where an indistinct form lay limp, its head hung over the ledge edge, forlornly.

"I don't know, Alex...maybe, it's...it's...IT IS!!!...It's a Makalu Snow Leopard!"

"Let's Goooooooooo  *!!!*"

Leopold's voice echoed, in boomerang fashion about deep chasms, and the children giggled...more reverberations sounded as Leopold hollered triumphantly, one more time...

"Let's......GOOOOOOOOOOOOOOOOOOOOOOO
OO!!!!!!!!!!!!!!!!!!!!!!!!!!!!"

The kids leapt into action.

"Que Podemos hacer, Leo?", Alexandria wondered, wrinkling her nose ponderously. The poor cat looked miserable, but, raised its eyebrow, questioningly, at the upright boy, who stood over both of them. She sat beside the leopard, stroking its head, softly, as the injured animal licked its damaged paw.

"I have an idea, Alex." He let loose his shrillest two-fingered whistle, piercing the blizzard's wrath with gusto, surprising the laconic cat even...and kept whistling and whistling, to the point nobody could tell what sound was real, imagined, or just a blasted echo!!!

Suddenly...their entrusted friend, the colossal, white-winged Albatross, appeared, snatched the snarling cat, and thrust forward, its broad shoulders heaving mightily against ferocious mountain winds…it rose up, briefly, as if climbing a steep roller coaster, then rocketed downward, like a jet fighter plane, drawing those magnificent shoulders inward for the rapid descent to the base camp animal clinic. **THE END**.

## Chapter Two

'A Sharkey Tale'

Alexandria and Leopold are scuba diving, when they happen upon an unfortunate scene...a gnarly fishing net, full of panicked creatures, struggling furiously for a way out, looking for any means of escape, imaginable. At the furthest edge of this massive net is a sad looking dolphin...and he knows what's "up"...hardly his first "rodeo", of a nautical kind...keenly aware, now, of the un-fathom-able dark, shadowy underbelly of a Super trawler...'Phantom of the Sea'...the intelligent dolphin has watched, tragically, his friends (& family, even!) hauled off to the 'Great Unknown', too many times...listened to the muffled, mechanized whirring sound, emanating from the monstrous ship, itself, of the net in motion being hauled in. The children's eyes are big as saucers, as they peer uncomfortably through their scuba goggles at the traumatized mammal. The creature's "smile" is the saddest smile Alexandria has ever seen, in this moment.

"Tenemos que hacer algo, Leo**!", Alexandria cried out, desperately.

"I'll <u>THINK</u> of <u>SOMETHING</u>, Alex", came his uncertain reply. Of course, he had no clue, but, to admit THAT would break the little girl's heart.

Just then, the kids *spin on a dime*, and face an approaching figure moving like a submarine, moving at a freight train's steady clip, its tail waving from a distance as if extending a greeting, and as it nears it looms ever-larger, slowly coming into focus. Bubbles bubble excitedly from the children's mouthpiece, and just as the Great White fish happens purposefully upon the net...WHAT HAPPENS? The prisoner fish ALL STOP...stop moving, entirely...and the mighty shark explodes through the netting, its sharp-as-a-knife-dorsal fin shredding it with the ease of a spider's web hand swipe (& do NOT try THAT at home...as spiders are pretty cool arthropods, and enjoy spinning their amazing habitats!)…..the massive swarm of fish make a beeline for the exit, and the kids hop on Felippa the Dolphin's back, for a nifty, free ride back to shore!!!

**THE END**

# Chapter Three

## 'Barely A Cub'

A little baby bear sat, *frozen* in fear, in a tree, surrounded by a raging forest fire, wind-whipped flames tickling its furry toes. Two little firefighter's stand at the base of the tree looking up, all geared up.

All three watch as the inferno flashes, wild-like, as another comes crashing down loudly, streaks of flame shooting like fire arrows at their heads. They duck. The bear cub whimpers.

"Tenemos que salvar al oso bebé, Leo?", his sister pleaded.

"Okkkay, Ummm...<u>save</u> the...Right! Let's see what we can <u>DO</u>!"

Leo yanked the oxygen tank off his back, tossed his trusty ax, handed his yellow helmet to his sister, and flew up the tree like a skilled lumberjack monkey, tossing <u>ALL</u> caution to the wind.

The pint-sized cub eyed him warily, keeping one eye fixated on his movement, and the other, peripherally, on the eerie orange glow engulfing the forest… 'Barely' *yipped*, baby-like, as Leopold grabbed him……and just then…to their utter astonishment, IT happened!!! The boy firefighter felt a cool drop on his brow…then another, and another, and the cub looked skyward, feeling a fat pearl of rain splash dreamily in his own eye, and the sky opened suddenly in a miraculous gush-a thunderous downpour it 'twas-and boy and cub flew down the giant Redwood, thoroughly drenched, 'Barely' wrapped tight in Leopold's one free arm.

Alexandria splashed merrily at the muddy base, as squirrels ducked back in their own trees, and chipmunks rolled chestnuts, playfully, chittering amongst themselves, like the happy forest creatures they were! **THE END**

## Chapter Four

### 'The Albatross'

To say our *mythical* giant albatross-the beneficent, winged creature, who gave the kids a "lift" out of a raging hurricane-has some unique, otherworldly abilities, is to state the obvious. Like a bear who poops in the woods, staying the course, if you will.

Alexandria and Leopold travelled near and far, after their rescue, finding themselves in all sorts of places around the blue and green globe...and everywhere they went, they seemed to find someone-whether human or animal-in need of some help. They wanted to do as the albatross did for them.

"Por qué estan solos estos ninos, Leo?", the little girl asked. "I'm not sure why they are alone, Alex", was his concerned reply.

A brother and sister from Syria sat alone in a field in a cold drizzle, unprotected from the elements. They were the same age as Alexandria and

Leopold, but they looked hungry and exhausted. Their own parents seemed nowhere to be found.

"Donde estamos, Leo?

"I believe we are in Turkey, Alex."

The four children gazed at each other, wondering who was what...or, where? The little Arabic girl, Bibi, asked her big brother Bilal, "Ayn nahn ya?" He shrugged. He had no clue where they were. All he knew was one thing...it wasn't home.

In no time a crowd had assembled. They were all filthy and hungry and too tired to travel any further...in a strange unwelcoming land, with no homeland to return to. Their beloved Syrian city had been destroyed by strangers who cared nothing for their safety, their homes all reduced to rubble.

Alexandria and Leopold were transfixed. Waves upon waves of these foreigners, big and small, young and old, criss-crossed this unplowed farm field looking completely lost, lost in the fog, looking like ghosts...cast off from humanity, hopeless...in a moment that    seemed like an eternity.

"Que Podemos hacer, Leo?", his sister wailed.

"What can we do?" he replied. "What. Can. We. Do."

In this blink of an eye, something unusual happened. A giant cloud of dust swept across the farm field, causing the multitude to turn their back, shielding their eyes, as the cloud roared in their midst. It stung, like a million pin pricks engulfing them. The children were afraid. The long, arduous journey to this barren landscape was enough...but, THIS seemed impossible-until it wasn't.

When the dust storm cleared and the crowd reopened their eyes, they all gasped, in sheer disbelief! The field sparkled like a trillion diamonds. A lake had appeared, blue as crystal...and fruit trees...trees of every variety...avocado, fig, and peach. Silver fish leaped from glistening, sun-splashed waters, and great geese chased, honking madly after the children who rushed toward the coolness of the spring-fed water. Parents gushed with relief, knowing once again...if only in the moment's time...and hopefully, longer...their children were saved.  **THE END**

## Chapter Five

'Sailing the Mediterranean Sea'

Alexandria and Leopold thought it would be nice to take a break...and have a vacation! Trekking about the globe doing acts of heroism and kindness toward others was difficult work, and they were tired, tired, tired. One kind gesture is deserving of another, of course, and they happened upon an elderly gentleman from Greece-alone in the world-with nothing but a large sailboat to keep him company...and, sooooooo......they climbed aboard!

They were drifting about one day, under a clear and calm, sunny, blue sky...blue as the breaching whale they watched, merrily performing an acrobatic act before their very eyes! A perfect day, it was, to relax ...or, so they thought.

"Que es eso?", Alexandria asked her older brother, squinting in the glare of the bright, midday sun. Leopold peered in the direction of her pointed finger and spotted an unshapely thing bobbing in the near distance, a water craft of some sort, not unlike their own...or, so he thought. As their sailboat drew closer, 'tho, it became apparent this was no ordinary boat taking a leisurely cruise. It was a mess, a misshapen, underinflated rubber dinghy with many "passengers" on board, all yelling and screaming, desperate for help, it seemed.

"Hay tanta gente," Alexandria cried out.

There were so many, in fact, Leopold began counting heads.

"Ellas estan perdidas!", she cried, again, tears streaming down her face.

Leopold realized, in an instant, his sister was right. These people were, indeed, very lost. They were from a dark-skinned continent, miles off the Libyan coast.

The gentleman Captain, carefully, maneuvered his sailing vessel toward the distressed dinghy. A child fell overboard, suddenly, squeezed over the side by the crush of humanity piled on top of each other. A mother shrieked in anguish. Leopold reached out and grabbed the little African girl by her arm, pulling her quickly into their own craft. Another child fell overboard, and Leopold reached out, again, pulling him on board, successfully...and again and again.

Before the sun had set on this eventful day, the three sailors had made many new *friends*-a whole boatload, in fact! As dusk fell on to a lilting, Mediterranean sky, a steady breeze kicked up, carrying the craft, steadfastly, along toward shore, in the most positive way, and they all dined, by candlelight, on sardines and crackers.  **THE END**

## Chapter Six

### 'White Giraffe'

White giraffe, you say?

What about the coat of many colors?... a patchwork of chestnut, orange and black, interspersed with wisps of white hair, I should say.

Little Alexandria curled up in the warm grass of a Kenyan savannah. She was tired after all the travel, and harrowing adventures. She laid her head on the neck of the motionless mother giraffe and looked skyward. Leopold stroked her baby's torso, softly, shedding a tear.

"Podemos salvarlos también, Leo?", Alexandria whispered.

Leopold choked up a bit, for this time he really had no answer for his big-hearted little sister.

"We are too late to save them, Alex. What is done, cannot be undone."

Thoughtlessly mean men with guns, called *poachers*, killed the last remaining white giraffe female on the planet, along with her calf. Only a single, solitary male bull remained...anywhere.

Leopold shut his eyes to avoid the sight of silent vultures circling overhead. He imagined, instead, flocks of flamingo and Saddle-Billed Stork, long-legged bird creatures, standing serenely in open, shallow water. This made him feel better.

When he opened his eyes, he noticed a fuzzy-headed Speckled Mousebird perched on his chest. He smiled. His sister was fast asleep, now, dreaming of butterflies chasing each other around an old oak tree. All was not lost, after all, in the Animal Kingdom. **THE END**

## Chapter Seven

### 'Going Home'

The giant, friendly albatross released its mighty talons, and the kids tumbled on to the glimmering beach. Gentle, white-capped waves lapped the shore, as a radiant sun shone brightly over the Puerto Rican Trench. It was a glorious day in the Caribbean Sea. They gingerly brushed sand off their arms and blinked at the sky. Then they noticed a familiar couple standing nearby, waving at them.

*"Tia Angelique !!!", Alexandria yelped.*

*"Tio Hector !!!", Leopold cried.*

Their aunt and uncle smiled, adoringly, as the children darted into their arms, for a big hug. What a journey it had been, and, now, for the meantime, anyway, the journey was over!  **THE END**

## 'Sampson Hoards Another Nut'

Sampson's not only a larger-than-life flying squirrel in the forest, known aptly as "Sampson's Forest", but, from all general appearance, seems to grow larger by the day...and why is this, I wonder?

Why, in a forest filled fantastically with fabulously furry, and, <u>friendly</u> I should say, creatures of all kinds, on land, air and water...why, when nature works in harmony, providing that which sustains life, to share and share alike, that is...is there one auspicious character, one big old rascal Sampson, behaving so scurrilously-slippery like a garter snake-taking not just what is meant for him, but...OTHERS, as well, you may wonder?

BECAUSE...SAMPSON...LIKES...TO...HOARD...NUTS!!!

"Nuts to that!" Charise the cherry chipmunk chirped cheekily, in a squeaky little voice.

"Who does that big bully think he is?"

Boscov the timid bear offered in a gentle, deep baritone.

Amidst the clamor and cacophony of the unruly forest family, assembled noisily ...no...<u>angrily</u> ...against their better nature one should say, at Old McDaniel's run-down meeting place, a mighty shriek stilled the air, from the back, suddenly!

138

The already anxious animals shuddered, and rafter pigeons swooped, aloft, rapidly to the opposite end, leaving ...a splotch here...and a splotch there...on the dusty floor that went...PLOP! It was the barn owl's call to order.

"Aye Aye-Hear Ye Hear Ye"

A rather odd-faced creature Bartoli is, some in attendance thought. Face shaped like a heart and cinnamon-tinged. Then...a throatier, guttural, sound...loud and deep...noticeable like a bossy dog. A Great Horned-Owl ...*There was an owl liv'd in an oak, the more he heard, the less he spoke, the less he spoke, the more he heard, O... if men were all like that wise bird...*

"*WHo-ho hoo hoo hoo*"

*...rare is the hare to escape the sharp talon snare, a mole seeks a hole this all seems so droll- how 'bout some rice? wouldn't that be nice surmised the mice? in a short span of time figured to be thrice...*

"*Hoo-h'HOO-hoo-hoo*"

The animal collective stood in rapt attention, immoveable.

*Winged-tiger in flight-what a sight in the starry night-Eyes glowing yellow a bird of prey is anything but mellow-Got to feel sad for the poor little fellow…*

"We are honored tonight to have a special guest," *Owsley the Orator* began. "A rarefied woman of dignity and aplomb, one who travels near and far, won't be bottled up in a jar." The crowd chuckled.

'The Honorable One', as he was also called, was a familiar, feathery, patchwork presence, and, before the clock of time had slowed his large frame, quite a formidable one as well…one that was always THERE in time of need, who carried himself with self-assurance and made the forest family laugh.

"Not a time to be haughty, nor cynical," Owsley continued. "We have a serious matter that needs to be <u>straightened out</u>!… and, why, may I ask, will the prevailing winds of time serve to bring forth a breeze in the leaves-not to appease-but, more so to please and bring ease to our glorious trees? ...why again?

The assembly jumped at the chance, shouting in unison.

"Because today's mighty oak is just yesterday's nut, that held its ground!"

"*Corrr-rrrect!!!!*" Owsley bellowed back.

".......and...*Whoooooo*...spun        primordially from the "big soup" of God's amazing kaleidoscope of cacophonic characters, bringing forth a symphony of delightful, if not, at times, <u>frightful </u>sounds...dwelling in our enchanted ancient  forest mosaic...who, may I ask, can strive to thrive amidst even the endangered beehive...?"

"We Can!" thundered the crowd.

Charise, the diminutive cheery chipmunk stood silently, front and center, her cheeks about to burst.

"Hush...hush, now," said the portly patrician, raising his broad wings.

The crowd quieted.

Owsley grimaced, as he raised a monocle to his right eye, squinting out at the crowd to read a simple proclamation.

"We of the forest, suffering the ravages of drought and flash-fire and, now, thievery from one Sampson the Colossus…"

"HOARDER!" the crowd yelled.

"…a finer fellow in better days," Owsley continued, "but, now, in desperate times, taken it upon himself to rob and plunder, to sweep all that remains to sustain us, from the deer and wild turkey, to the rabbit and opossum, to the wood duck, woodpecker and bobcat quail…"

Charise, the pint-sized granary accountant, shifted uneasily, inspected her inventory heet, woefully, then turned to face the anxious audience, expecting the worst. "We have no acorns left," she announced. A muffled groan filled the dusty air.

"Exactly!" Owsley exclaimed, strangely nonplussed, it seemed, considering the dire straits of the moment. The forest, you see, was in a terrible conundrum. "Is why I have summoned from a far away, quite majestic and mythical land, one of soaring ice-capped mountains,

142

shimmering blue lakes and sweeping, verdant valleys……yet, a land not so unlike our own, and, in fact, quite similar in a forest way…welcome our esteemed cousin and visionary…Shirina!"

From behind the assembled assemblage flew in her majesty, a stunning, barrel-shaped, Eurasian Eagle Owl. Fiery orange eyes, and the glistening sheen of a feathery coat… "Look at that wing-span!" gobbled Tom, arching his head backward to catch a glimpse of this apparition, flying stealthily overhead. His saggy neck stretched taut, for a change. Shirina, winged-wonder of the Himalayas, born of the valley Kathmandu, in an enchanted place called Nepal Mandala…land of the Newar's…

The crowd gasped at this phantastical sight, shining like Tiresias, with eyes that blazed Tantric-of an anomalous vortex beam, you may imagine-sprung from the tree of life, itself. Devata of devatas, of a feminine mystique, Shirina is, celebrating nature's divinity, smack dee dabble in the center of that Shakti Cluster *cosmic order* rabble-babble.

A hushed silence was broken by the squeaky voice, front and center.

"We just want our acorns back," Charise, the cheery-cheek chitter chat quipped, standing erect with little paws on her hips, looking slightly unimpressed- dissatisfied, even! ...by this glowing spectacle, now parked next to Owsley.

"Yeah!" goaded Gordie, the oft times, garrulous *pocket* gopher, visibly shaken, mid-drift in the mob... "Whom...I mean <u>WHAT</u> is this sight before us...or, shall I say... <u>THING</u>...?"

Other voices chimed in, wondering aloud where <u>THEIR</u> precious acorns had disappeared to, and before you knew it, the whole blasted barn was a gaga again, wings flapping, sows gruntin', crows crowin'...a loud, bell-clanging mess of mutinous misery, raising a ruckus, so to speak.

"Our children don't have food."

...and, then, Shirina began to speak, in hushed, measured tones. The ruckus stopped.

"The land where I'm from, a very distant land from here, is not so unlike your own," she began... "A land, it is true, beset and besieged by much struggle, sadness and desperation, of late...when our fair Mother Earth shook and everything came tumbling down."

There was a murmur in the room.

144

"But" she continued… "We are not so unlike your own, in a magical way, too!

The valley of Kathmandu is, also, the land of maple and elm and beech and spruce, in the deciduous forests and conifer hills. We have trees of flagrant beauty that bloom in spring…the violet jacaranda…yellow silk …solandra…wild orchids and Sacred Pipal, along the Ring Road."

The kindly, soft-spoken Shirina reached inside her silver-shine of feathers and pulled out a flower of Rhododendron, ceremoniously, reaching out to Charise. The littlest chipmunk accepted it and smiled.

"There is a much loved story, a children's story, told from one generation to the next, among the Newar's, called 'The Sparrow's Lost Bean' she continued. "A tale of a hungry bird who discovers a bean, and then finds it missing. Exasperated and feeling lost, she enlists the help of a king riding atop an elephant, yet, no one she approaches seems to listen, nor care…until the sparrow encounters a single solitary ant.

Owsley raised a feathery eyebrow.
"Perhaps some of you recall a visit one year's past, when my brother, Siddharta came to visit. An *Eagle* same as

myself, naturally, and much like our *cousin* Owsley, the Great Horned Owl... see."

"Well, Siddharta had heard of this big old flying squirrel Sampson, and kind of wanted to have a talk, but, he found times weren't so tough in your forest, at that point in time, anyway, and he returned to the Mandala...<u>but</u>, times have, indeed, gotten much tougher, now, and Sampson much bigger, and something had to be done...

"Something <u>HAS</u> to be done," chittered Charise.

"Sooooooo...Siddharta returned to your land, a short time ago, leaving behind the tiniest sprig of bark from the fairest of trees, called the 'Ginkgo Biloba', or, "maidenhair"...a two hundred and seventy million year old tree! He dug little holes in the ground, dropped the bark, then covered them up overnight. Ginkgo Biloba sprung up everywhere!...and, especially around  Sampson's favorite Black Oak Tree...BUT, they weren't to be seen by the naked eye-they were  invisible! Imagine an eighty-foot tree bursting yellow saffron, in autumn's magical foliage ...that...is...invisible!" Shirina surveyed the mesmerized crowd, moving her head, all the while, and blinking...then continued.

"Naturally, Sampson flew off his branch, gathering ALL the acorns from the forest floor as fast as he could, and ate as many as he could, in the fastest time possible, while hoarding the rest in his own, shady, hollowed-out oaken granary, he selfishly called "Mine & No One Else's"...and he did this day after day, contentedly, leaving none for no other, in a pathetic  way.        "WHAT...HE...DIDN'T...KNOW..." BUT...WOULD...SOON...FIND...OUT

"Was if one eats too many acorns too fast and for too long... ...one goes completely crazy!" The forest animals burst out laughing at that. A good comeuppance couldn't happen too soon for their hoggish-minded hoarder.

Sampson the Colossus, as we speak, was now outside Old McDaniel's barn, doing unimaginable flips and flops, convulsing like a kooky canary completely out of his *tree!* Boscov the Bear barreled through the large barn doors, and the whole excited lot followed, into daybreak, now, to see

147

what this all about. Owsley and Shirina swept to the loft, for observation's sake.

Sure enough, there was the hoarding hurricane himself, spinning like a spinning top...tossed like a giant *spraddle-dee-docked* squirrel caught in a tornado's tumult, making all kinds of unearthly sounds, in the process!

The forest creatures crowded around him in a circle, watching the spectacle in amazement. After a while, they began to feel kind of sorry for the big galoot, suffering so much unfathomable agony, which is when Shirina (on a wing-and-a-prayer) handed Charise a spike full of vitamin cure. The chipmunk, unhesitantly, jabbed the tail whirling flipper-flopper in his big ol' butt!

Sampson came to his senses, then, only to find the whole of the forest having a big chuckle...a big, collective belly laugh, in fact...at his expense, for a change! Shrunken down to size, as they say, to that of a regular squirrel, for pete's sake...and, most importantly...friend, once again, to his many furry, feathery & even <u>scaly</u> friends, elated to have him back!

...and as they watched the friendly Shirina flap her wing..."So Long"... and, fly  stealthily away...they noticed a forest filled with the "maidenhair", and all the "silver fruit" they would ever need.   **The End**